Alien & Possum

Friends No Matter What

by **Tony Johnston**

pictures by **Tony DiTerlizzi**

Simon & Schuster Books for Young Readers

New York London Toronto Sydney Singapore

For Kevin,
dear, sweet possum of an editor.
And for all the possums who have landed
in my trash can.
—T. J.

To the memory of Arnold Lobel—May your words and pictures
hop into many a young mind for years to come.
—T. D.

SIMON & SCHUSTER BOOKS FOR YOUNG READERS
An imprint of Simon & Schuster Children's Publishing Division
1230 Avenue of the Americas
New York, New York 10020

Book design by Anahid Hamparian
The text of this book is set in 20-point Bembo.
The illustrations are rendered on Strathmore plate bristol board, in "Winsor and Alien" brand watercolors
and gouache along with "Possum Prismacolors" colored pencils.
Printed in the United States of America
2 4 6 8 10 9 7 5 3 1
Library of Congress Cataloging-in-Publication Data
Johnston, Tony, 1942-
Alien and Possum : friends no matter what / by Tony Johnson ; illustrated by Tony DiTerlizzi.
p. cm. Summary: Possum and Alien become friends and find that they have both
similarities and differences.
ISBN 0-689-83835-2
[1. Opossums—Fiction. 2. Extraterrestrial beings—Fiction.
3. Friendship—Fiction.] I. DiTerlizzi, Tony, ill. II. Title.
PZ7.J6478 Al 2001 [E]—dc21 00-045065

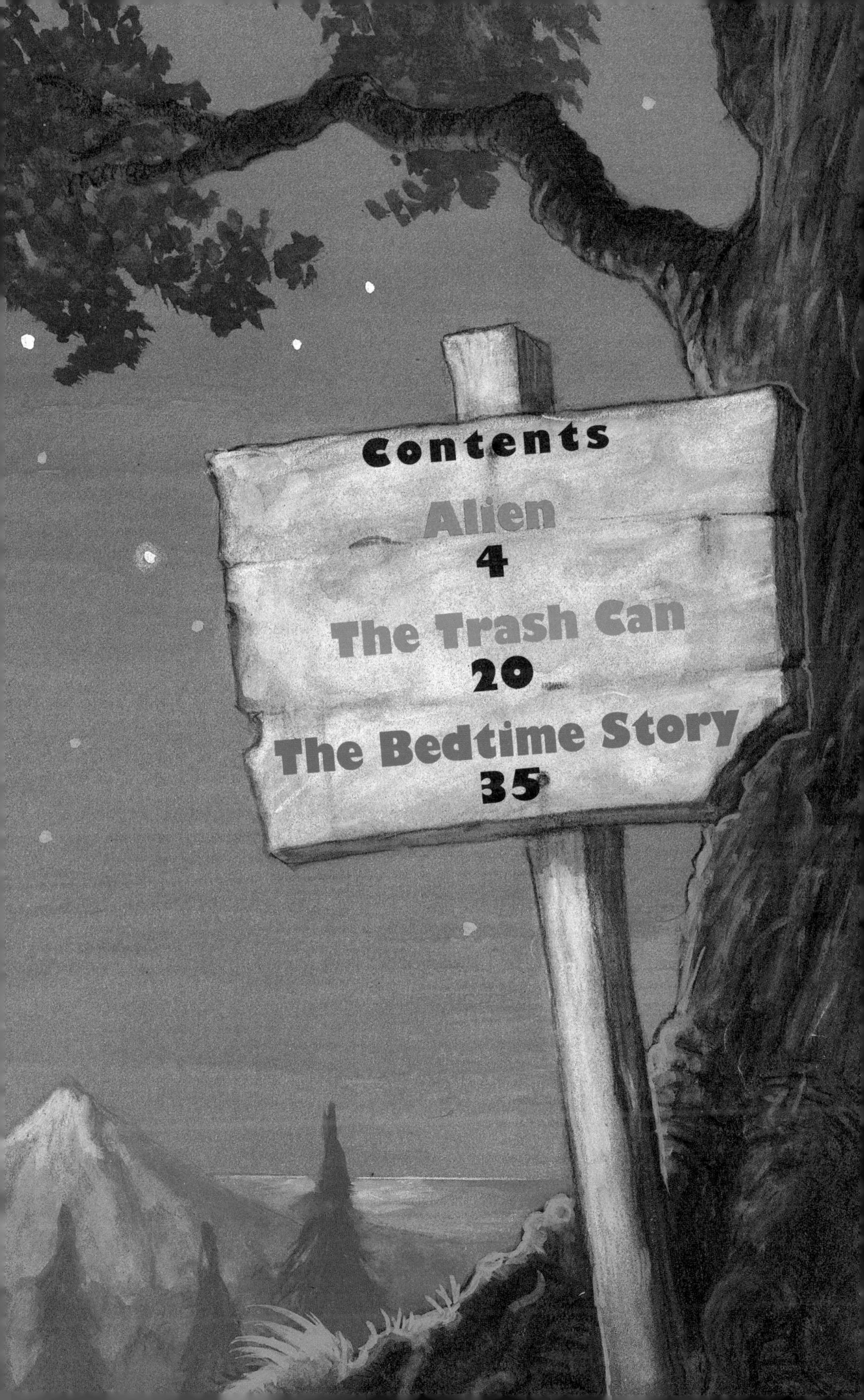

Contents
Alien
4
The Trash Can
20
The Bedtime Story
35

Alien

Possum loved to stay up late. One night he was outside enjoying the stars.

A star fell. No, it was a spaceship.

"Oooh," said Possum. He looked close.

4

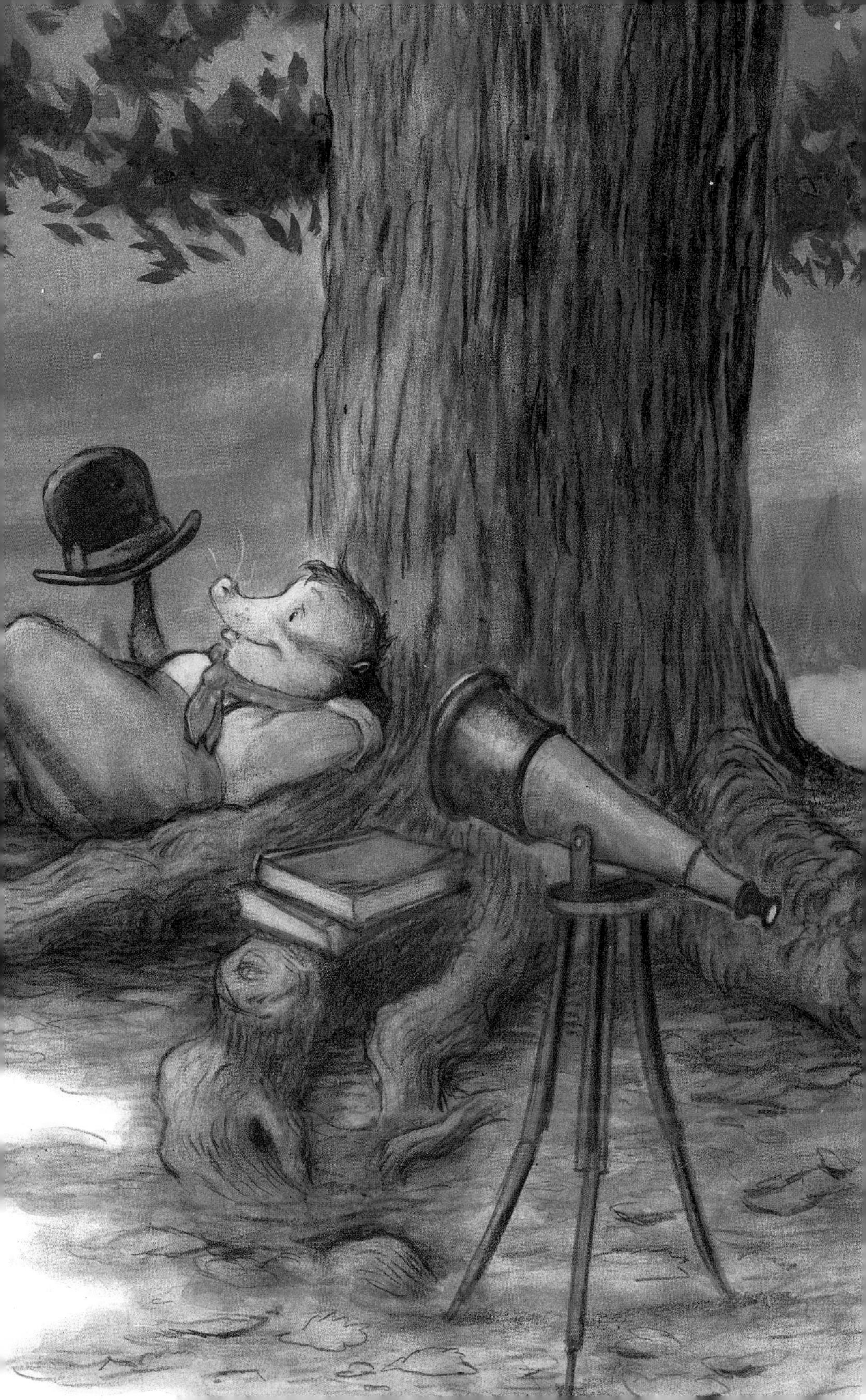

Dit-dit-dit. A space creature came out.
It was made of many strange things.

It made many strange sounds.
Wreench. Creench. Cronk.

Possum made a strange sound too.
"OOOOOOH!" said Possum.

The space creature got scared.
WREENCH! CREENCH! CRONK!
It screeched.

Then it ran away. *Dit-dit-dit-dit-dit.*

"Stop!" cried Possum. He ran after it.

It did not stop. *Dit-dit-dit-dit-dit-dit-dit.*
It ran faster.

It ran among the trees.

It ran behind a tree and hid.

"Where are you?" called Possum.

"I am far away," said a close voice.

"Are you here?" asked Possum.

"No, I am not here," said the voice.
"I am gone."

"That is too bad," Possum said. "If you
were here, I would be your friend."

"What is a friend?" asked
the voice.

Possum said, "Someone who
likes you no matter what."

"But we are not the same,"
said the voice. "You make
strange sounds.
I do not."

"What strange sounds do I make?" asked Possum.

"Strange sounds that go 'OOOOOOH!'" said the voice.

"Anyone can be friends," Possum said.

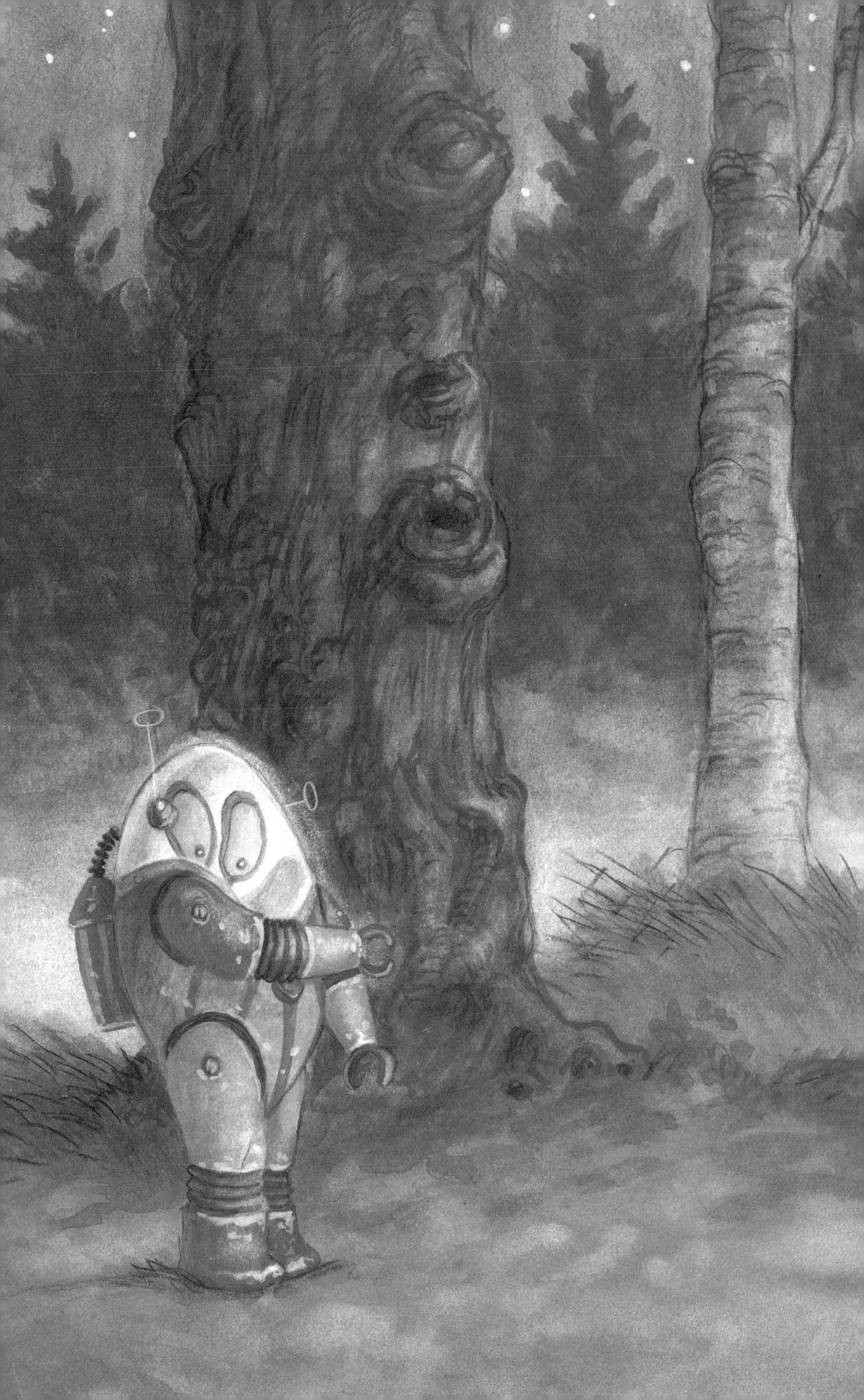

"You are hairy. I am smooth,"
said the voice.

"We can still be friends,"
Possum said.

"I am many colors,"
said the voice.
"You are no color at all."

"I am gray," said Possum,
"the color of a rain cloud.
Things of all colors can be friends."

"Goody!" cried the voice.

Dit-dit-dit. The space creature came out
from behind the tree.

"I am Alien," it said.

Possum said, "I am Possum."

Alien walked up to Possum and hugged him. Possum hugged Alien back.

"We are friends," they said together, "no matter what."

Then Possum said, "Alien?"

"Yes, Possum?"

"You make strange sounds too."

Wreench. Creench. Cronk. Alien laughed.

Then they went home to
Possum's tree.

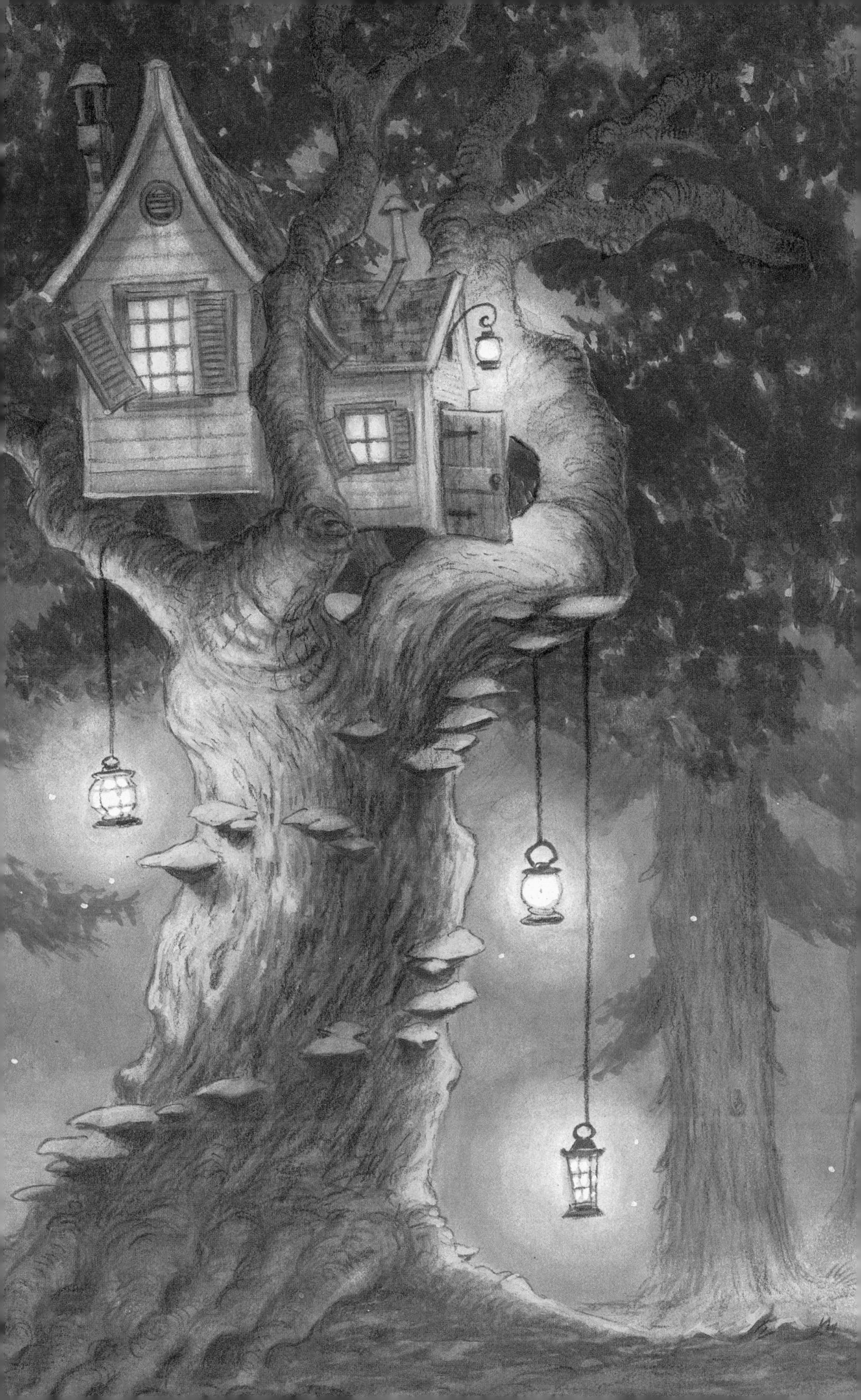

The Trash Can

One night, Possum was hungry.

He said, "I need a snack, Alien.
Let's find some trash."

"What is trash?" Alien asked.

"Trash is something delicious,"
said Possum.

"Like high voltage?" asked Alien.

Possum groaned. "No, Alien. Like
potato skins. And cold oatmeal.
And old fish heads. This is what
delicious is."

"Oh," Alien said.

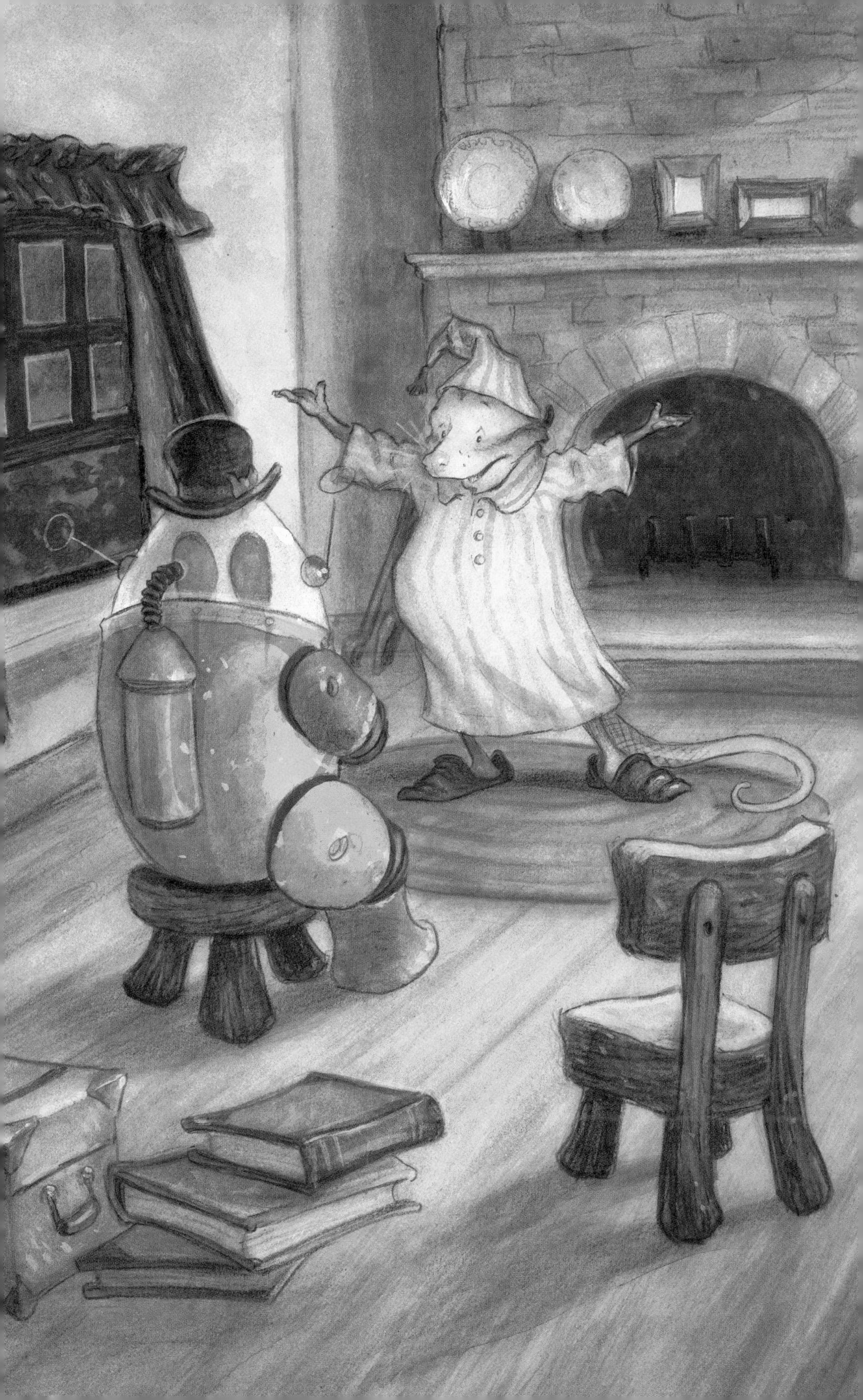

Possum led the way.

Dit-dit-dit. Alien followed.

Sometimes they looked for falling stars.
Or the moon.

Mostly they looked for trash.

All the time Possum sniffed.

"You are making strange sounds,
Possum," said Alien.

"I am not," Possum said.
"I am sniffing."

"Sniffing sounds silly," said Alien.

Possum said, "Sniffing is the most unsilly thing there is, Alien. Sniffing helps me find trash."

"Oh," said Alien.

Sniffing helped Possum find trash.

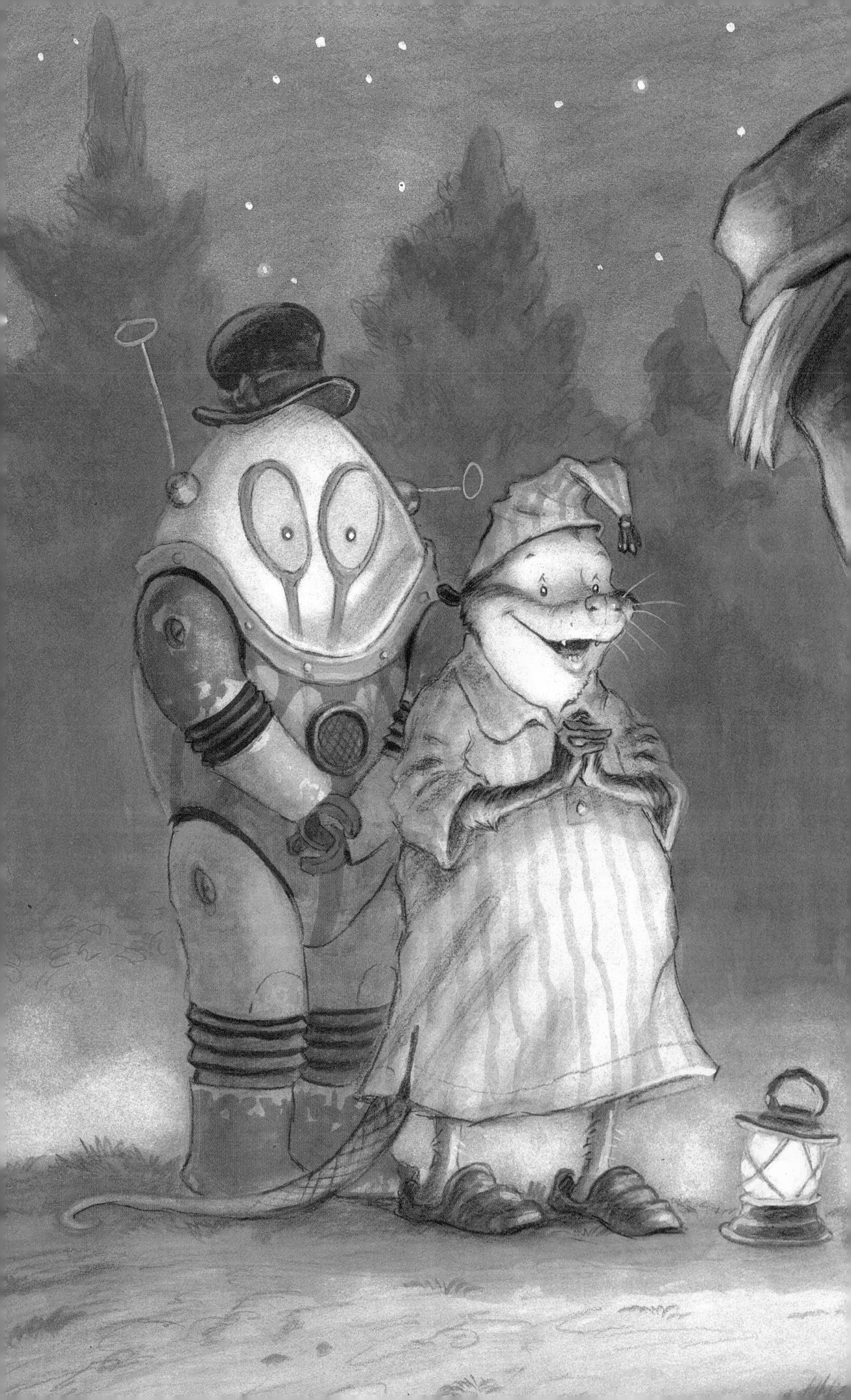

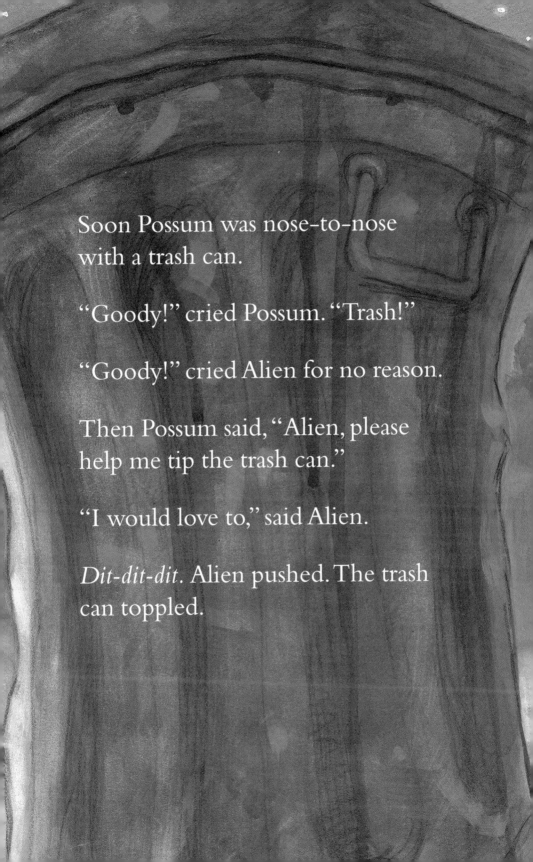

Soon Possum was nose-to-nose
with a trash can.

"Goody!" cried Possum. "Trash!"

"Goody!" cried Alien for no reason.

Then Possum said, "Alien, please
help me tip the trash can."

"I would love to," said Alien.

Dit-dit-dit. Alien pushed. The trash
can toppled.

"Thank you, Alien," Possum said.
He began to nibble trash.

Alien did not nibble trash. It did not
nibble anything. It looked at the trash
can. It liked the trash can.

"Hello," said Alien.

The trash can said nothing.

"Hello," said Alien.

The trash can said nothing.

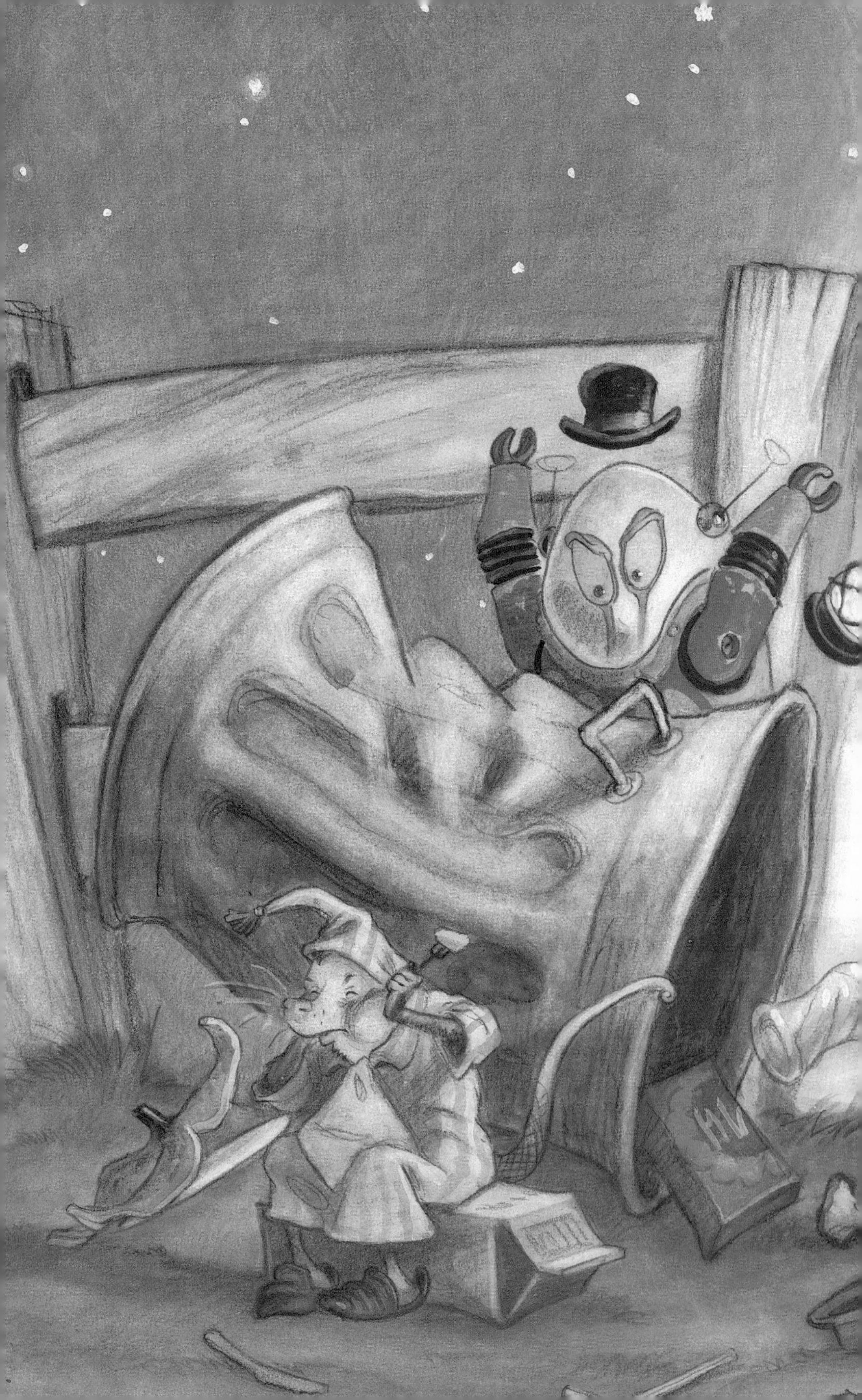

"HELLO!" shouted Alien.

The trash can did not say a word.

DIT! Alien bumped it. Alien gave it a big dent.

The trash can was quiet.

Alien was loud.

DIT-DIT-DIT-DIT-DIT! Alien bumped the trash can many times. Alien gave it many dents.

"It is too loud to eat!" shouted Possum. "What is the matter?"

Alien said, "This trash can will not say 'hello.'"

"Alien," said Possum, "trash cans don't talk."

"Oh," Alien said.

Alien sniffed very loudly.
Then it walked away. *Dit-dit-dit*.

Possum was not hungry anymore.
So he followed Alien home.

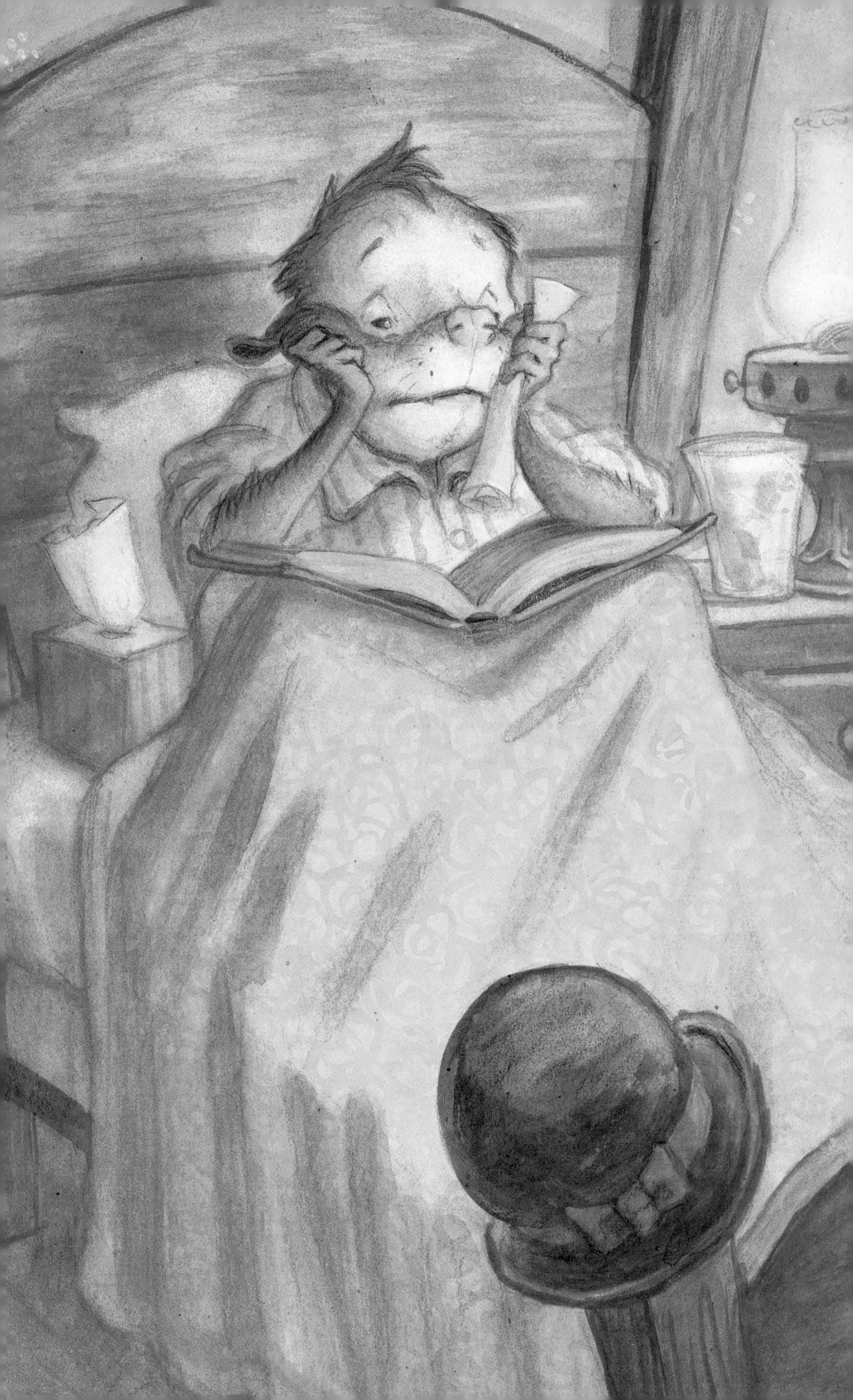

The Bedtime Story

It was late at night.

Possum was in bed.
He was reading a book.
He was crying.

His tears were falling
on the pages.

"Why are you crying?"
asked Alien.

"I am reading a bedtime
story," Possum said.

Alien said, "It must be sad."

"Very sad," Possum said. "It is the
saddest bedtime story I know."

"Why?" Alien asked.

"Because it makes me droopy,"
answered Possum. "It makes me drowsy.
It makes me fall asleep."

"But Possum," said Alien, "aren't bedtime
stories for falling asleep?"

"Not at the beginning!" cried Possum.
"I always fall asleep too soon. I never
know the end."

"Then give me the bedtime story,"
said Alien. "I will read it to you.
Maybe that will keep you awake."

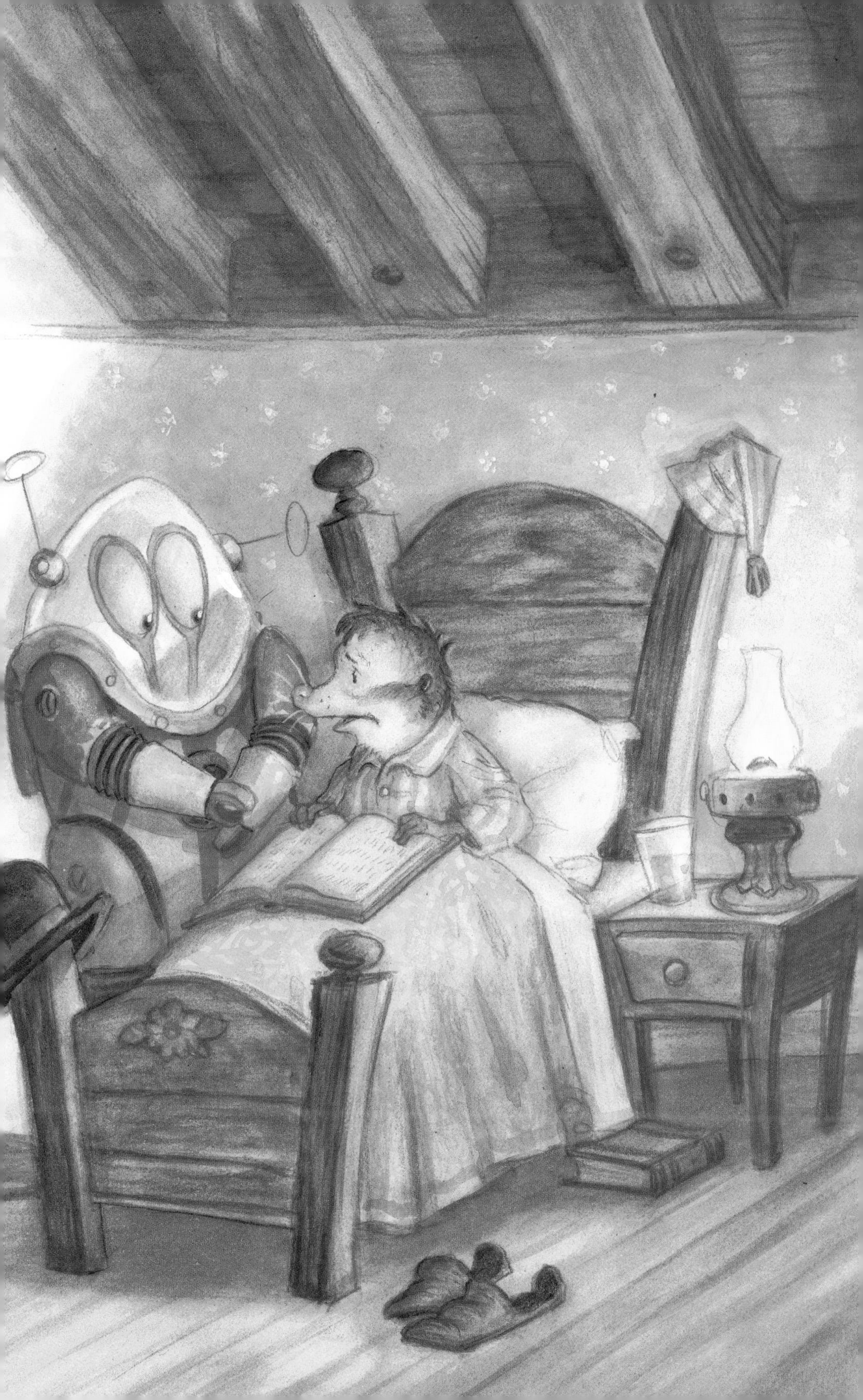

"Okay, Alien," Possum said. "Read the bedtime story to me. But if I fall asleep, please pinch me."

"Okay, Possum," Alien said. "I will be glad to pinch you. But what if you still sleep?"

"If I still sleep, please put ice down my pajamas," Possum said.

"Okay, Possum," Alien said. "I will be glad to put ice down your pajamas. But what if you *still* sleep?"

"Then, let me sleep," said Possum.

The bedtime story was soggy with tears.

Alien read it anyway.

Possum listened.
He drooped.

He drowsed.
He fell asleep.

"Wake up, Possum!" said Alien.
"You are missing the bedtime story!"

But Possum went on sleeping.

So Alien pinched Possum.

Possum went on sleeping.

So Alien put ice down Possum's pajamas.

Possum went on sleeping.

So Alien let him sleep.

Possum woke much later. He cried, "I missed the end again!"

Alien said, "I tried hard to keep you awake."

"Did you pinch me?" asked Possum.

"Yes, I did," said Alien.

"Did you put ice down my pajamas?" asked Possum.

"Yes, I did," said Alien. "Then I let you sleep."

"Why did you do that?" Possum screamed.

"You told me to," said Alien.

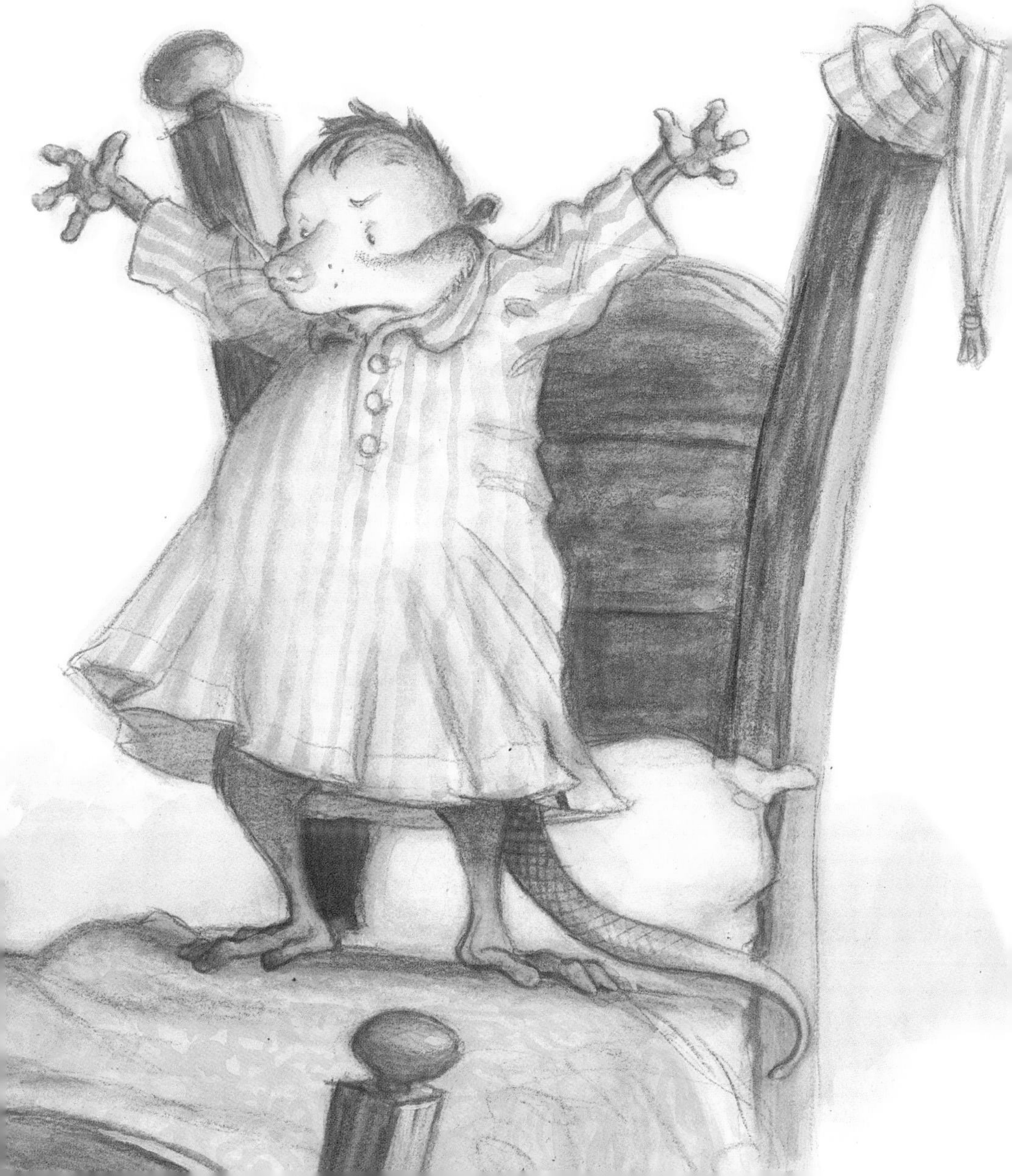

"Then read it to me now," said Possum. "I am wide awake."

"I cannot read it to you now," said Alien. "The book is gone. It was such a good bedtime story I ate it."

"Oh." Possum drooped like a wilted flower.

"Don't be sad," Alien said. "I know the whole bedtime story."

"You do?" asked Possum.

"Of course," said Alien. "I have an electro-perfect memory. And I did not fall asleep."

"Will you tell it to me now?" asked Possum. "While I am wide awake?"

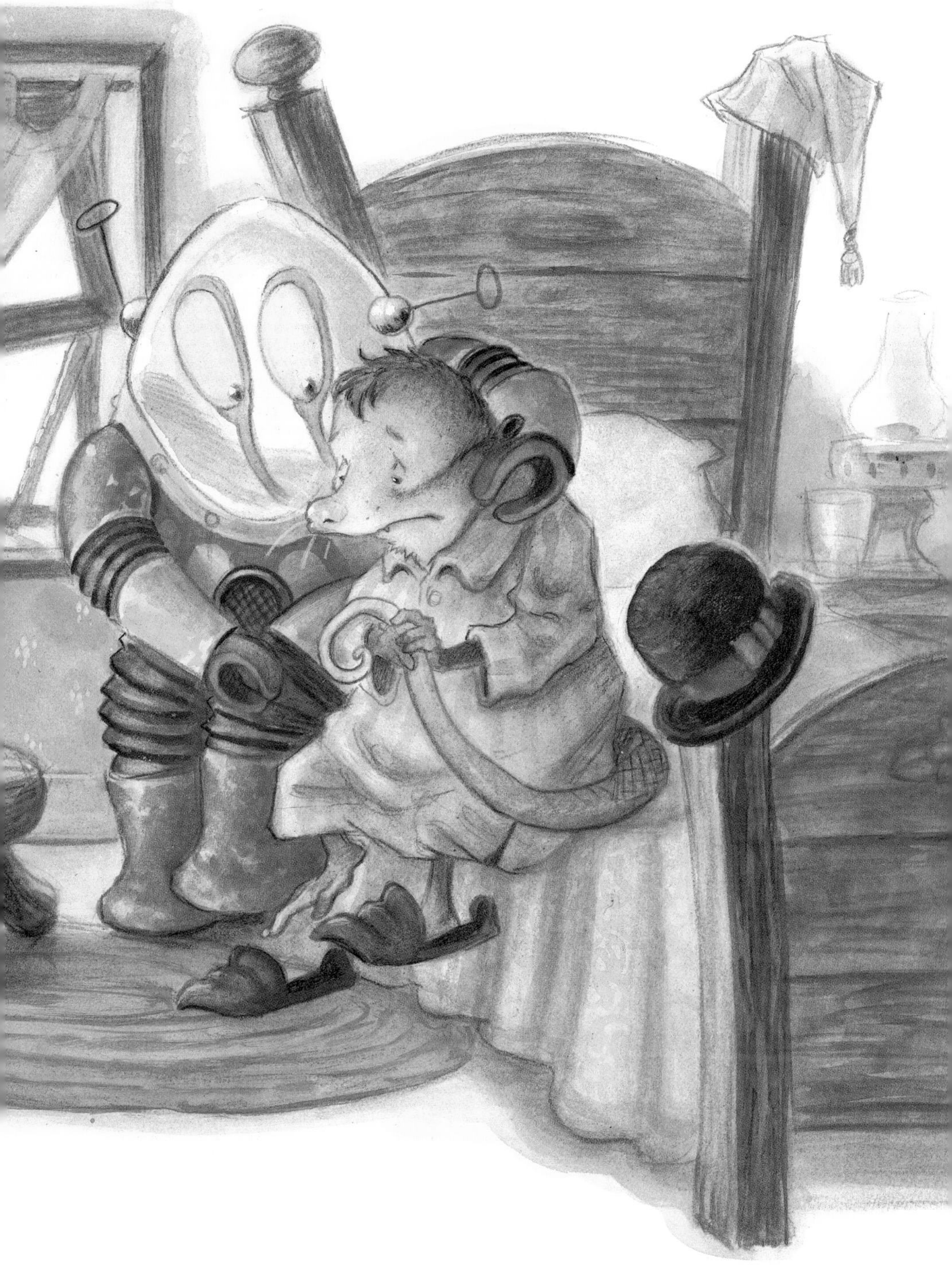

"Of course I will," said Alien.

"Goody," said Possum.

So Alien told Possum the bedtime story in the daytime. In the sun. And Possum did not fall asleep. He heard it to the very end.